THE WoLF AND THE SHADoW MONSTER

Avril McDonald

Illustrated by **Tatiana Minina**

Crown House Publishing Limited
www.crownhouse.co.uk

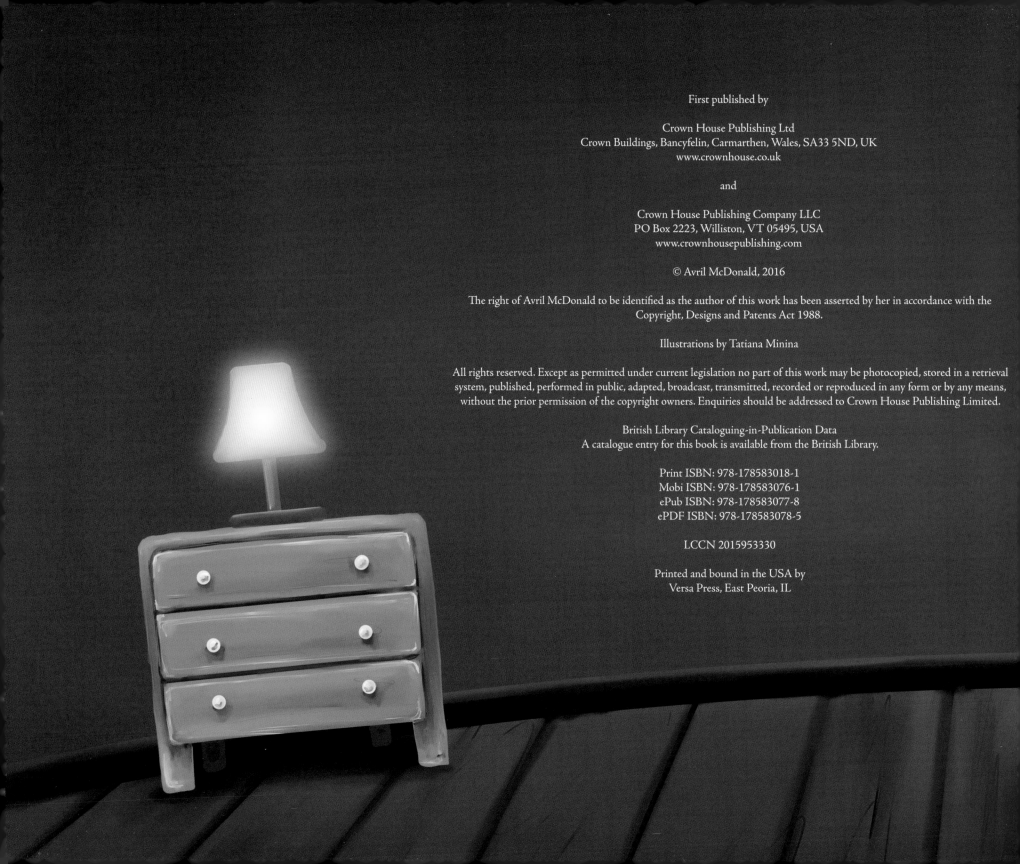

First published by

Crown House Publishing Ltd
Crown Buildings, Bancyfelin, Carmarthen, Wales, SA33 5ND, UK
www.crownhouse.co.uk

and

Crown House Publishing Company LLC
PO Box 2223, Williston, VT 05495, USA
www.crownhousepublishing.com

Illustrations by Tatiana Minina

British Library Cataloguing-in-Publication Data
A catalogue entry for this book is available from the British Library.

Print ISBN: 978-178583018-1
Mobi ISBN: 978-178583076-1
ePub ISBN: 978-178583077-8
ePDF ISBN: 978-178583078-5

LCCN 2015953330

Printed and bound in the USA by
Versa Press, East Peoria, IL

For my mum and dad, who showed me that when there's love in your heart, you're as brave as can be!

Thanks to Åsa Pettersson for her inspiration and contribution to Feel Brave's work and to the poet Robert Saxton for his editorial directive.

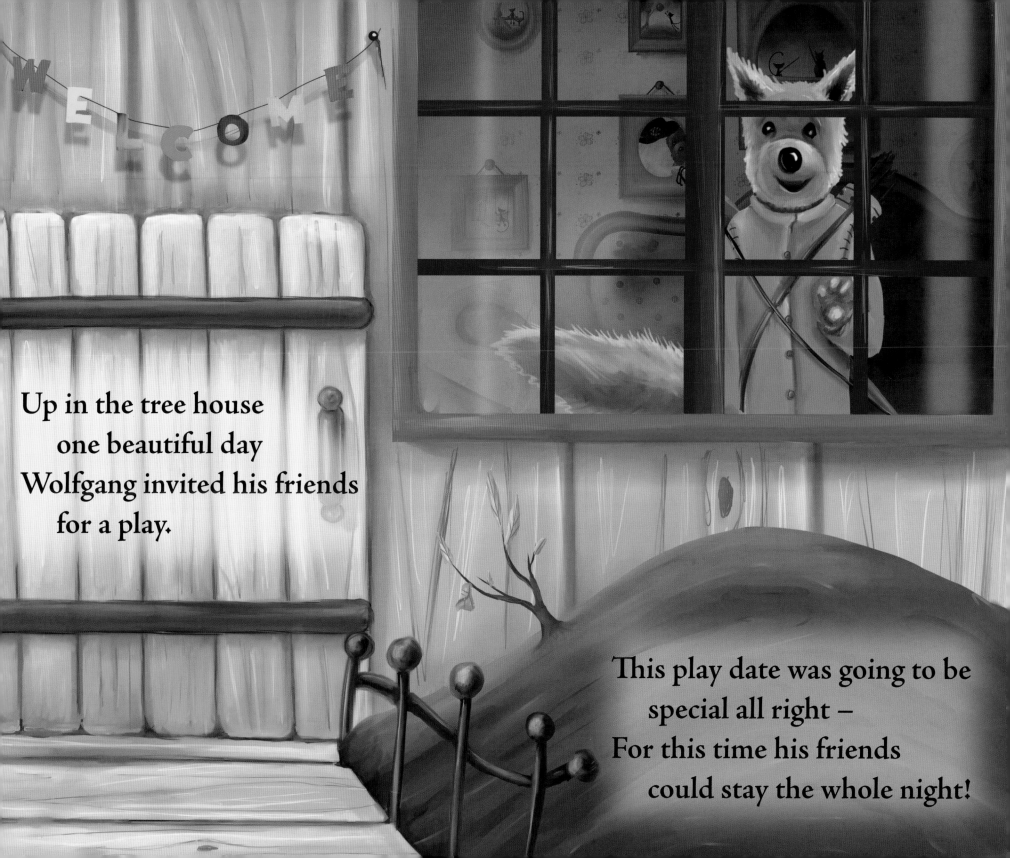

Up in the tree house
one beautiful day
Wolfgang invited his friends
for a play.

This play date was going to be
special all right –
For this time his friends
could stay the whole night!

Catreen arrived first
with her favourite bear.
Montgomery made sure
he brought clean underwear.

Along came the monkeys
with cookies to eat
And then Daisy Pig ...
with high heels on her feet.

Wild games began
    as they danced and threw balls
And jumped on the chairs
    and climbed up the walls.

They laughed and they squealed –
what fun they all had!
But when the lights were turned off,
the play date turned bad.

In the dark poor Wolfgang
   felt nervous and scared –
He had a big problem
   that hadn't been shared.

He tried to forget it
   and hoped it would go …
But problems like this
   aren't that simple, you know.

The owls were surprised
when he let out a shout:
"Turn the lights on!" he yelled.
Wolfgang's secret was out.

His friends started laughing,
    which made him feel sad.
When they poked fun at him,
    he began to get mad.

"Wolfgang," they said,
    "you're a big scaredy-cat!
We all love the dark,
    what's your problem with that?"

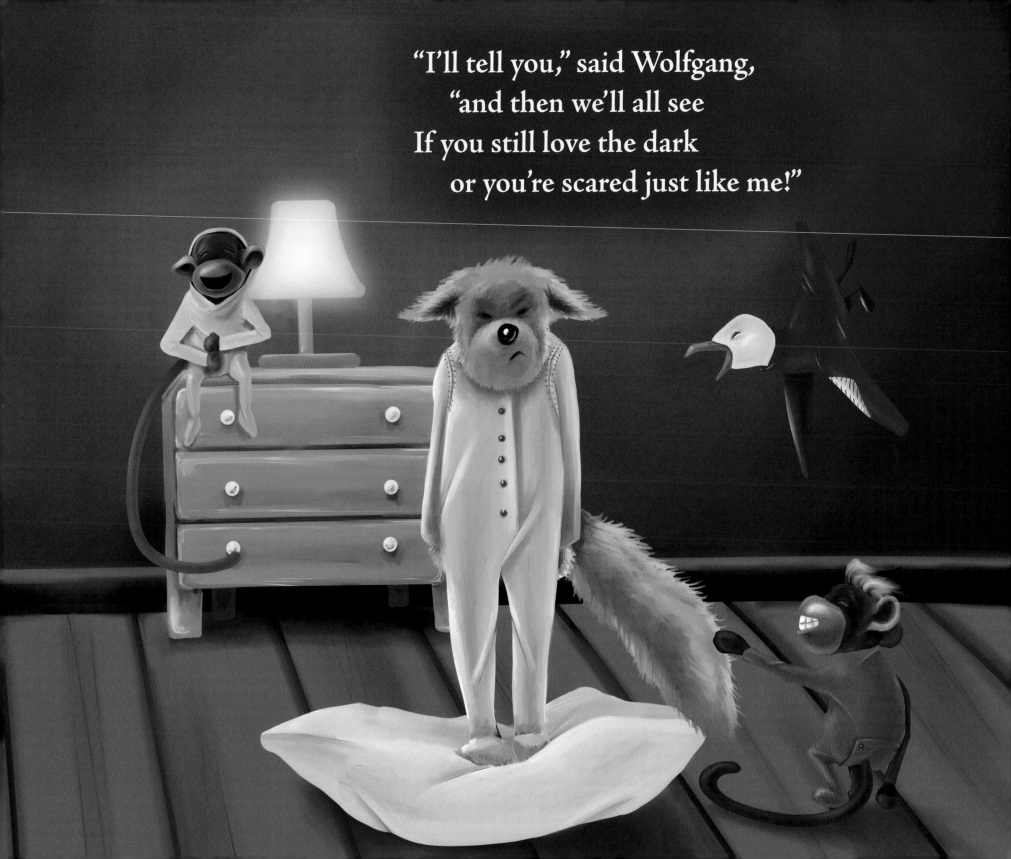

"I'll tell you," said Wolfgang,
"and then we'll all see
If you still love the dark
or you're scared just like me!"

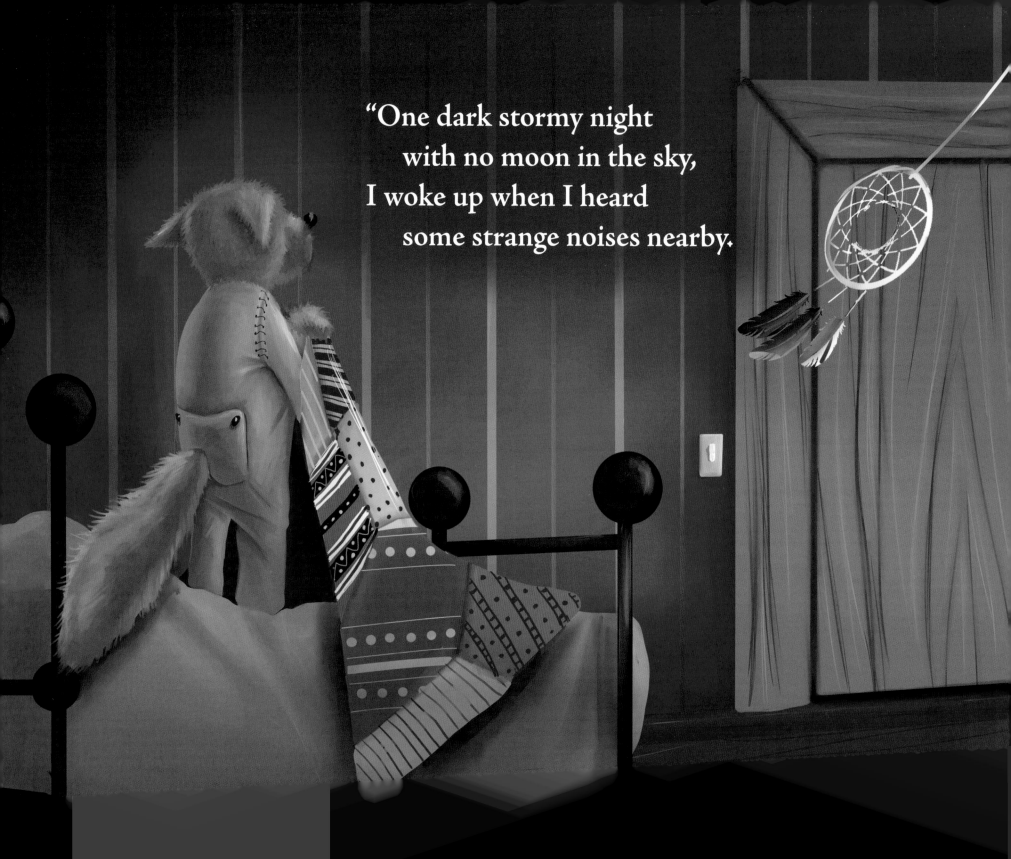

"One dark stormy night
with no moon in the sky,
I woke up when I heard
some strange noises nearby.

Then out of the shadows
   I got a surprise
When a monster appeared
   right in front of my eyes.

I tried hard to scream
   as I ran to the door,
But no sound would come out –
   that's not happened before!"

"I was shaking with fear
      when I turned the light on ...
But the light must have scared it:
      the monster had gone.

And now when it's dark,
      I just know that it's near ...
And I have a bad feeling
      it's followed us here!

Wherever there's darkness
the monster will hide."
"Shhhhhh!" said Catreen,
"I hear something outside!"

They all froze with fear.
No one knew what to do.
They did NOT love the dark!
Now they were scared too!

At the worst moment ever,
    their night light just died.
Then the monster appeared.
    So they trembled and cried.

Their screaming woke Spider,
	who knew what to say:
She had a good spell
	to make bad go away.

"My dear Wolfgang," said Spider,
	"if only you knew:
There's a powerful magic
	that's deep inside you.

So if something is scary,
	or cruel or unkind,
You can change how you feel
	with your magical mind.

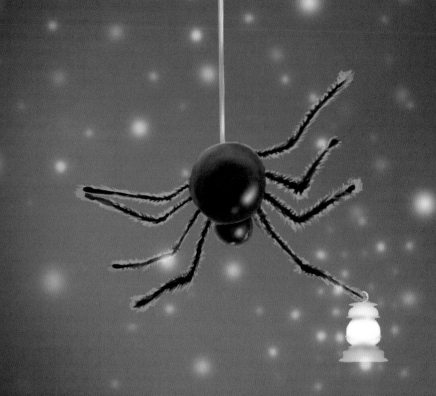

Just take a big breath,
  feel brave and stand tall.
Imagine it's funny …
  or cute, and quite small.

Have a try for yourself,
  I think you might see,
With your magical mind,
  you're as brave as can be!"

Wolfgang was fearful
 of trying this spell.
He was feeling so scared
 he felt quite sick as well.

But he also felt fed up
with feeling this way.
And his friends got a shock
when they heard Wolfgang say ...

"Hello Shadow Monster,
    it's nice to see you ...
I've got some new magic
    that I'm going to do.

I'll take a big breath
    and then make you quite small.
You don't have to worry,
    it won't hurt at all.

I'll give you big eyes
and some lovely soft fur.
There'll be no more strange sounds:
from now on, you'll just purr."

Then they watched with surprise
as Wolfgang breathed in.
When he let his breath out
they saw magic begin.

The monster got smaller,
like Wolfgang had said,
And it turned into something
quite lovely instead.

"What a trick!" said Catreen,
"Now let me have a go!"
So she tried it on Bruno,
who frightened her so.

Montgomery decided
that he'd like a try.
So he made the loud thunder
sound small in the sky.

Daisy Pig said,
"Clarissa is nasty and mean!"
Then she made her so small
she could hardly be seen.

The monkeys all thought
that the spell was such fun,